MY AUSSIE PLANTS AND ANIMALS

Illustrated by Cat MacInnes

Avocet

Acacia Seed

Dingo

Dianella

Echidna

Eucalyptus

Greater Bilby

Grevillea

Ibis

Illawarra Flame Tree

Jabiru

Jagera

Lorikeet

Lilly Pilly

Numbat

Native Thyme

Platypus

Pigface

Ringtail Possum

Riberry

Sugar Glider

Silver Dollar Gum

Tasmanian Devil

Tulipwood

Ulysses Butterfly

Umbrella Plant

Velvet Worm

Vitex

Willie Wagtail

Waratah

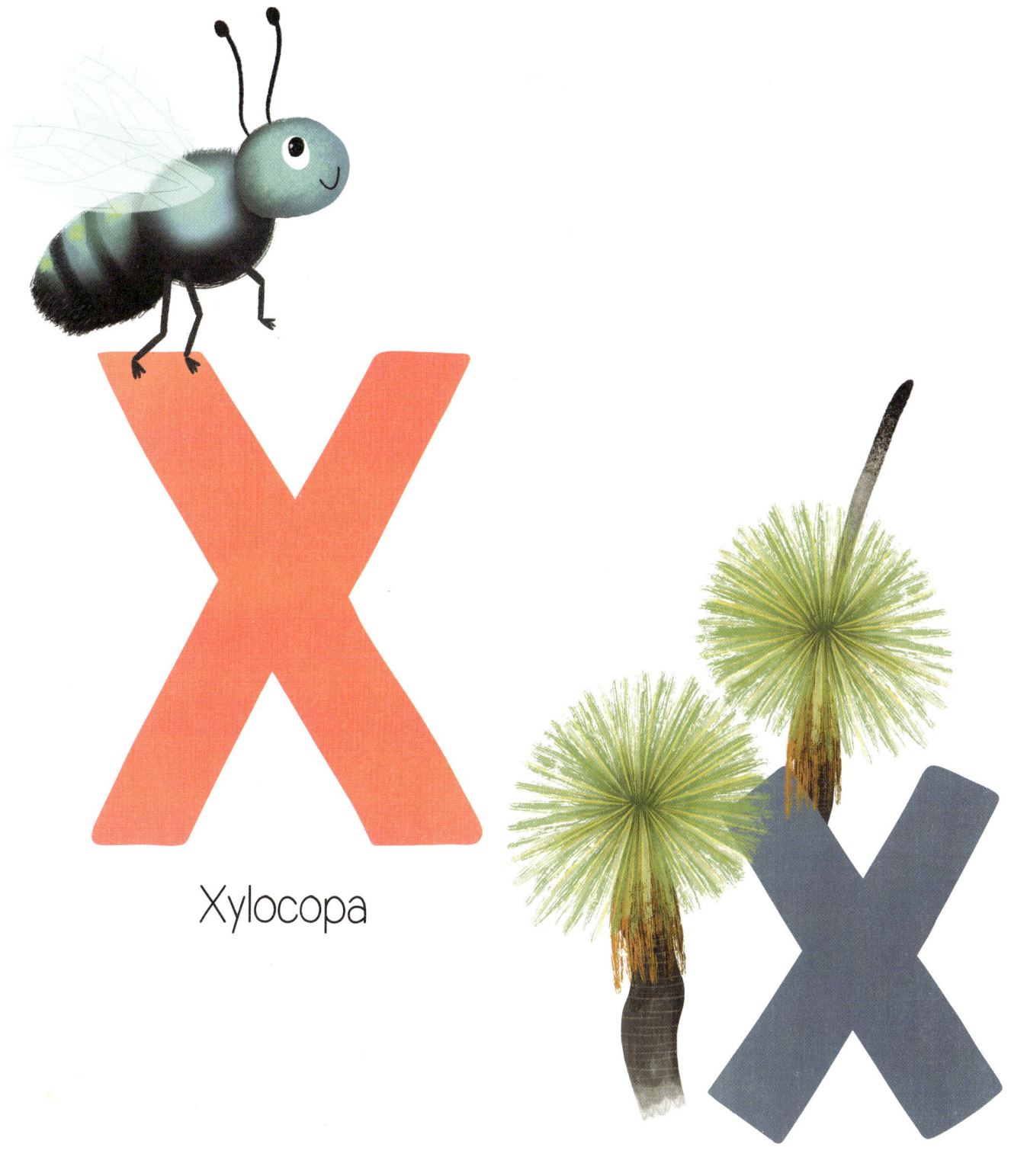

Xylocopa

Xanthorrhoea

Yabby

Yam

Zebra Finch

Zena

To my little family,
for being the sweetest Aussie
creatures I know. CM

Cat MacInnes is a freelance illustrator, based in Melbourne. Born to an artist father and ceramicist mother, she was always going to be into art. Her works are gentle and whimsical, with use of strong bright colours and polished vectors. Cat illustrates all sorts, including; books, greeting cards, magazine covers and portraits (of people AND pets). When Cat is not working, she likes gardening, thrifting, and sticking googly eyes on things around the house! But mostly Cat loves hanging out with her family, and her little dog named Fizzy.

First published in hardback in 2022
by Windy Hollow Books

PO Box 265, Kew East, Victoria, Australia 3102
www.windyhollowbooks.com.au
www.facebook.com/windyhollowbooks

Text copyright © Cat MacInnes 2022
Illustration copyright © Cat MacInnes 2022
The moral rights of the author and illustrator
have been asserted

This book is copyright. Apart from any fair dealing for the purposes of private study, research, criticism or review permitted under the Copyright Act 1968, no part may be stored or reproduced by any process without prior written permission. Enquiries should be made to the publisher.

ISBN: 9780645323535
Design by Nuovo Group

A catalogue record for this
book is available from the
National Library of Australia